Miss Pheromone

Miss
Pheromone

Collins Odhiambo

Published by Sahel Publishing Association,
a subsidiary of Sahel Books Inc.
P.O. Box 18007—00100
Nairobi, Kenya
Tel: +011-254-715-596-106
For questions and orders log on to:
www.sahelpublishing.net

A Sahel Book

Editor: Sam Okello
Interior designed by Hellen Wahonya Okello
Cover designed by Hellen Wahonya Okello
Printed in India, U.K., U.S.A.

To my country Kenya

TABLE OF CONTENTS

Chapter 1

The giant euphorbia tree provided a lovely shade for the young men of Hera village. By early evening, the shade would already be extensive; and still it steadily spread over the short green grass. There, the young men sat to say anything about anything and anyone.

And there they were even today, seated in various relaxed postures. Most of them were in trousers, which were now drawn up their legs given their seated position. Some were in shorts, and one of these sat with his knees raised, so that his large and loose yellow pair of shorts revealed rather much of what should have remained completely hidden.

Their entertainer – or shall we say chairman – was conspicuously absent. Owiti always stood in front of his seated friends and played the much needed role of conversation facilitator. He was well known in Hera village and beyond for the dramatic fashion in which he had quit school. Owiti had gone in front of everyone during a school assembly, unauthorized, of course, and declared: "School is for fools." His schoolmates had watched with open mouths as he left them standing there, turning his back on them literally, leaving school, never to return. His teachers were to take several days just trying to find fitting words in which to express that dumbfounding happening. He, however, remained a champion of sorts to the villagers, owing to his strong personality. Now these friends of his clearly were missing his presence.

Someone wondered aloud where Owiti might be. Before any response, however, everyone turned at once to look at Bob, who was joining them unexpectedly and from an unexpected direction.

Hardly had Bob settled upon the grassy ground when he loudly complained to the gathering: "Some of us here are truly ill-mannered."

"In what way, Bob?" shot Andrea, who had earlier taken his time to read the graffiti upon the trunk of the huge tree under which they now all sat. A brief silence followed, creating quite some tension.

"I'm going to find out who wrote my name on the euphorbia," charged Bob, waving his forefinger in the air threateningly.

Andrea suppressed the urge to speak further, lest he should be singled out as a possible author of any of the allegations and insinuations.

All of a sudden, everybody rose and made a near mad rush to the foot of the tree to see for themselves what Bob was talking about. Andrea joined in the rush.

Well, it was not unusual to have such writings upon growing trees. As a matter of fact, there were several claims and other funny remarks etched upon this very trunk. What actually was interesting was that Bob had finally been dragged into matters of love; matters he always regarded as messy, scandalous and sinful. From such, he had done his best to keep his distance.

'Bob loves Miss Pheromone', declared the graffiti. Those in front read and read again as if what they had read was not actually written there. The ones standing behind them craned their necks, struggling to get their gazes past the shoulders and backs that crowded in front of them so obstructively, nudging and urging their owners to allow them too to see what was written. The letters had been scratched into place with the sharp edge of a stone, or something of that sort. The milky sap had not quite dried, and had managed only a short-distance flow down from each letter, before getting congealed up.

They all read the piece of allegation in utter disbelief, shaking their heads in unspoken wonder as to why Bob, of all people, was being smeared with such mud. Was it not common knowledge that Bob never liked girls? Or even if he did, did everyone not know that his father never would have entertained such nonsense, and that it would have been real war between him and his son Bob? But that aside, just what exactly did that person intend to achieve by this particular claim? Surely, some people were bad!

Onyiego, however, gave a new twist to all this. Turning to face away from everyone, he cupped his face in his palm and started sobbing. This took away the picture of the words which their memories had carried from the trunk of the tree right to their sitting places which they had since comfortably resumed. Onyiego had been left behind studying the words and was now joining the rest.

It was becoming more and more serious. Soon it was uncontrollable. Unable to keep standing, he collapsed into a heap, placing his head between his knees so as to sob even more. None knew why Onyiego was reacting so to graffiti that was not about him. Some derided him, saying a big person such as he was, and a man at that, was bringing upon all of them great shame by crying so openly. Another shouted out Onyiego's name, telling him to behave himself. Passers-by cast glances to the shade in an effort to make out what was going on there. Some stopped altogether, for Onyiego's loud hoarse voice now dominated the scene. The very curious passers-by made for the shade.

Onyiego cried on.

Now, if the rumour that Apidi was eying Miss Pheromone had stressed Onyiego, this new development concerning Bob might as well have sent him into a depression. Why on earth was everybody after the very girl he wanted? This was what was hurting Onyiego; and he was actually now rolling upon the ground, never wishing to be touched by anyone or to listen to any words of consolation. They had no idea what he was going through; so, they could not be at a position to calm him down, his heart told him. They just had to leave him alone, he felt.

Soon enough Onyiego was carried shoulder-high by his friends. He had to be taken away from there for he was causing a commotion. A sizable crowd had now formed and more and more people were heading to the shade, including village women and girls who were bearing barrels full of water upon their heads.

Physically strong he may have been but together his friends had over-powered him. On they trudged towards his place, Onyiego wiggling within their tight hold of him.

When they approached the gate to his place, he asked them to allow him to walk – perhaps keen to keep his father out of these affairs of the heart, especially if they could reduce a young man to a mere baby such as was the case now. They yielded to his request but guarded him closely just in case he should once again go berserk and run amok.

When he had got into the compound and was now heading to his personal hut, the friends left the gate from where they were watching him. None of them went back to the shade that evening.

Onyiego never slept that night. He had never taken supper, a turn of events that had, inevitably, come to his father's attention. To those his father had sent to him to make inquiry, Onyiego had submitted that he was so unwell that he needed no disturbance whatsoever, not even medicine, much less so food. They had left him alone; after all, his seemed more of some deep annoyance at something than actual bodily illness. Nevertheless, they remained alert. One could never really know what could occur out of a seeming non-issue such as this one.

By about midnight, Onyiego got up. He felt around for his box of matches, and got it. He struck a match and lit the tin lamp. He sat back upon the bed holding his chin contemplatively. For a couple of minutes he remained so. Then he rose and reached for a notebook. From the middle of this he plucked paper. He got a ballpoint pen and settled at the little table in the room in order to compose a love letter.

There he was! He might misspell quite a bit, and his handwriting might not be the best in the world, he wrote in the opening lines. Also, his choice of words might not be anywhere near being Shakespearian. But his love for Miss Pheromone, he declared, surpassed what even the best language ever could express.

On he wrote to his girl; the only one who could have him laugh to the extent of falling to the ground; the only one for whose sake he had forgone food and was now forsaking sleep. God knew that Miss Pheromone was beautiful and that her beauty had stirred up everything in him; that he would never be at peace with himself till the day his heart would find a place in her heart.

Onyiego was well aware of instances where a girl, on receiving a letter from an admirer, read the same only to reduce it to tiny pieces before sending the miserable remains back to the owner, with an oral message that she did not like jokes. There were even more humiliating actions. Such were specially premeditated and discussed by the girl in question and her female peers, with a view to causing real damage to a young man's romantic ambitions, and to his ego generally. None of these possible setbacks, however, would receive much of

Onyiego's attention. He looked at the roof, telling himself that a soldier going to war neither doubts his ability to fight and win, nor engages in discouragement of whatever nature.

His wrist watch showed that it was already two o'clock in the morning. He placed his written expression of love between pages of a magazine over which he then placed the pen he had used. Between then and dawn he would lie in, just looking forward to being with Miss Pheromone and making known to her the precious contents of his heart.

Chapter 2

The sun was already up in the sky. Onyiego, having read and re-read the love letter, delivered it to his object of affection. He did this personally, lest a messenger should play tricks on him when he was serious enough to forgo food and sleep for the sake of love.

Miss Pheromone held the letter, looked at her name on the white envelope and smiled. She could sense that much thought and courage had gone into preparing and delivering this apparently important message. Onyiego said to her that what he had to tell her was all in the letter. She responded that she would read it and then let him know what she thought about it all. He nodded as if this already was the consent of love that he craved from her. He turned to leave Miss Pheromone's grandmother's compound. As he walked away, he felt that he had left his heart in the girl's hand, literally.

Miss Pheromone had just returned from the lake, where she had gone to fetch water, and had been combing her hair, which had been pressed by a barrel full of water, which she had borne on her head from the lake. It was while she was making herself up so, just outside her grandmother's house, that she had noticed a young man coming in her direction. She had immediately recognized him, for he had carried her suitcase for her from the bus stop right up to the stairs of her grandmother's house three days before when she had arrived in this village. Her grandmother, an early riser, had gone to her cassava farm. The previous evening, before they had retired for a night's rest, Miss Pheromone had inquired from her grandmother what she could wake up to do the next morning. She had been told that she could go and fetch water from the lake for use there at home. Her grandmother normally went for water first thing. Having laid the water barrel in the kitchen, she went to the farm. With her granddaughter now taking care of the matter of water as well as general cleaning, she could move straight to the farm as she today had done. She was now busy planting cassava stem cuttings in the soil, laying them there obliquely.

Once through with chores, Miss Pheromone settled down at her favourite position in the living room, near the window, to read a novel. Up the wall opposite this position was the framed picture of her late grandfather, whom she never had the chance to see. He was a second-generation immigrant here in Hera. He had sired a girl of stunning beauty, who became the apple of his eye: Miss Pheromone's mother.

By late afternoon that day, she was out and about, meeting the villagers, chatting up those engaged in this or that little money-making activity such as petty sales services. Everyone liked her. Her skin complexion alone always elicited pleasant thoughts about her. The beauty of her face attracted. Her speech charmed. What she said truly endeared.

At the end of her social encounters out there, she got back to her grandmother so that they may cook and eat together while enjoying great conversation.

Then she would read by lantern light up to bed time. This particular day the last thing she read was not a novel chapter but the love letter she had received in the morning. Now placing the letter back into its envelope, she began thinking seriously about her promise to let the young man know what she thought about the content of the letter.

Well, he had written saying that he loved her very much; that until she admitted him into her heart, he would remain restless within himself. What really was she to tell him? What would admitting him into her heart exactly entail? Would he be satisfied just enjoying a good conversation with her every day? Would he not want something more than just this, just like any other man would?

Miss Pheromone now unfurled the white mosquito net hanging over her bed and began tacking it in along the edges of the mattress. As she did this, she thought more on what her response would be. She noted to herself that she was not too naïve to understand the ultimate desire of a man's heart. All the same, she reached a conclusion. She would not prejudge him but let him be friends with her. It would be an organic sort of friendship fit to calm the restlessness inside him. She would handle accordingly whatever he might further want from her beyond such friendship.

She turned the knob of the lantern lamp clockwise and anticlockwise, clockwise and anticlockwise again, raising and lowering the wick till its yellow flame went out. She got herself between the sheets in order to have a good night's rest, and nice dreams, if any would come her way. Her grandmother was already in the slumber land.

Darkness and quiet took full charge inside here as well as outside. The entire region was dead silent. One might say that this rural area was very many years away from being like the city. When would these people have the experience of a night club? What if, after a long day, one wished to be out there with buddies having a good time and saying things that keep them up to date with the affairs of the world? How about a night-long entertainment staged by celebrities, both local and international ones? Was it, therefore, any wonder that villagers were always slow and behind the news and modern trends? On a different thought, though, maybe it was all good that such should be the case. People needed to spend their nights sleeping after doing their very best of whatever they set out to do. Maybe it was not proper that city dwellers should turn the night into day without also turning the day into perfect night full of such wholesome rest as Miss Pheromone and everyone here in Hera village, for instance, were now enjoying.

Come dawn, Miss Pheromone would get up and do some reading, a habit her dad had cultivated in her by his own example. She would go to the lake to fetch water. Then she would have all the rural peace and quiet to read some more, talk heartily with friends and villagers and do whatever else she would like as a big girl on holiday.

Chapter 3

Fenny Pheromone was visiting her maternal grandmother's place for the second time in her life. She had been here years before, as a little girl with a flat chest. She had very much enjoyed playing naked upon the shore of Lake Hera, beside her cousin Mercy, who would then be bent there, cleaning cooking vessels and other utensils or, sometimes, clothes. Mercy had since been married, and their grandmother had since then mostly lived alone, for such grandchildren of hers as had come to take their basic studies here as a way of also keeping her company had, after some time, decided to return to their parents.

Fenny Pheromone was now a big girl sending men mad. She would have stood out even among other light-skinned individuals from anywhere in the world; thus, being the only one of her kind here, she completely captured the imagination of these villagers, who held that she was the model of feminine beauty.

Her father, Mathew Pheromone, loved her very much. What with the mollycoddling, the fashionable attires, breathtaking hairstyles, cash money, and all!

This December holiday, when she had expressed a desire to visit her grandmother, the father had raised no objection at all. He knew it had been long since she was with her mother's mother. Sugar, baking flour, cooking oil, salt, rice, toilet soap, bread and drinking juice were but a few of what made up her luggage when she arrived from the city for this visit to the village.

Now she was taking this village by storm. Her presence excited the entire village. Young men could not look at her and pretend that what they saw had no effect on them. Everybody else was amazed that someone should be so beautiful and so sociable at the same time. Perhaps the fact that she was so well-spoken could explain her preference for company. Many often adopted snobbish isolation as a mechanism for covering up their communicative inadequacy or the reality that they may not know much after all.

Indeed, urban girls loved to be heard. The flexibility of their tongues on languages other than the local ones, their grasp on current affairs, and all that, made them very loud when in company. Miss Pheromone was no exception. But this aside, engaging Miss Pheromone on a more serious note gave one the idea that she was not only well informed but also truly intelligent. As well, her English was thoroughly polished. How she achieved this in an urban linguistic environment that encouraged mixing of languages was part and parcel of the wonder that she was.

Miss Pheromone was in touch with the very latest in the entertainment circles: celebrity gossip, music albums, movies, you name it. It was from her that the village young people actually got to hear of such big names as James Bond, Denzel Washington, Angelina Jolie, Jenifer Lopez and so on. As to those who were too famous to escape even the villagers' notice, Miss Pheromone was now in the role of narrator of minute details of the lives and affairs of such. One such truly famous individual was Michael Jackson. Miss Pheromone could describe even how, when, where and why he made love; and in graphic detail!

Miss Pheromone also dismissed those stars who did not appeal to her. And since she had monopoly over information concerning these particular individuals, the village boys simply adopted her attitude towards such celebrities, of whom they themselves, of course, knew next to nothing. For instance, in her conversation with Onyiego in her grandmother's living room two days after receiving his love letter, she had characterized Whitney Houston as the kind of woman who would go boasting to her colleagues at the lakeshore of how often she was hit by her husband, had she been married here in Hera village, that is. On hearing this particular comment, Onyiego had been truly impressed at Miss Pheromone's intimate knowledge of people whom he himself had known only in terms of their excellent music on the radio, and whom he revered for their amazing talents.

There was more for Onyiego to discover about this girl there in her grandmother's living room that mid-morning. When she tried Whitney Houston's 'I Have Nothing if I Aint Got You', Onyiego staggered in laughter and let himself fall onto the floor.

He rose, swearing that that was exactly the voice he listened to on the radio. Miss Pheromone watched him, smiling at Onyiego's capacity to express the fact that he was impressed.

Indeed, to be with Miss Pheromone was to discover a lot behind that beautiful face. It was little wonder, therefore, that many trooped into her grandmother's usually quiet compound. They wanted to learn from her. They listened to her great English. Some wanted the whole of her. Many a young man sought to be first-among-equals in her attention. She made each feel good about himself. But the one thing each privately wanted her to resolve was: who, among them, would be the bull that gets to sit alone in the big shade of her heart.

Chapter 4

Bob was a son of a pastor. (Such were referred to as PKs, pastor's kids.) The strict and absolutely Calvinistic upbringing in his father's household was taking a toll on him. He longed to do more with his life than just singing in church and listening to Bible verses repeated over and over. He longed to be a permanent part of the evening meetings under the euphorbia tree. He hated being tethered like a cow when his age mates went about freely enjoying their youth. If his spiritual faculties still remained loyal, the emotional ones clearly were already in an uprising.

Bob wished to have a girl, just like most of his peers had. However, he did not wish to have just any girl. He wanted Miss Pheromone! This therefore made his quest doubly challenging.

Having a girlfriend at all was something his father would not entertain in the first place. Being the one who gets to win Miss Pheromone's heart among so many determined competitors was the next trouble for him. And to know that he had hardly any experience in such matters!

In this girl, and only in her, Bob saw everything for which he had been yearning. He had experienced this sort of feeling the very day she arrived here this holiday. He had made to carry her suitcase for her but he had thought of what might be reported to his father and held back. Onyiego had then rushed in to offer the assistance. Damn his strict dad!

Miss Pheromone was only about his own age, Bob contemplated in his bedroom, yet she knew so much about the world. She thought of things so freely. She spoke of things so freely. And she did things so freely. In contrast, he himself was monitored right at the thought level. His father, for instance, would take his seat, which was so positioned in the living room as to give him a direct view through the open door and all the way down to the gate. Resting his back upon the seat, his right arm folded across his chest to meet the left elbow, he would caress his chin seemingly idly. As he did that, his gaze would focus on various things around: the roof, the furniture, those seated in the same room, those walking in and out, what was happening outside, his own feet, the wall clock labeled 'quartz', and everything else. Bob had come to learn that these were not by any means idle moments for his father. Many were the occasions he had rightly guessed what Bob was thinking of, almost accurately.

"But I am just seated here; I have not said anything. How do you know what I am thinking?" Bob had on one such occasion dared to grumble, reacting to his father's comment that he should stop thinking of girls, for they were a potential source of harm.

That grumbling from Bob had given his father the opportunity to expound on a chain of related Bible verses relevant to proving evil thoughts. He pronounced upon them boldly, connecting particular phrases to Bob's manner of walking, his tone of voice, choice of words, how he sat, the songs at whose tunes he whistled, his supposedly low level of religious enthusiasm as well as his general comportment and disposition.

He had gone on to counsel Bob that he should never think unwholesome thoughts; that the society had great expectations of them, being a holy family. This statement on expectations of the society was constant in his father's utterances.

Bob sat up upon his bed and revised the events at the big shade the evening he had appeared there unexpected. He smiled to himself, noting that so far he had succeeded in a big way in calling attention to the fact that he could be thought of as a contender in the race to Miss Pheromone's heart. It was for this reason that he, himself, had etched the words 'Bob loves Miss Pheromone' upon the trunk of the giant euphorbia tree. His friends needed to stop being shocked that he too could be interested in a girl. Further plans were to be even smarter and their execution truly foolproof. Shielding his father's interference in this whole matter had to be as important as any main strategy he would put in place. It was not lost on him that his father was more than capable of physical violence. His own mother had often been on the receiving end of his father's violence, and in his very presence. A fist fight with his father, of course, was out of the question. He would just submit and receive his due as his mother did. A mere rumour was all it would take for his father to descend upon him with blows. Girls, his father's rule remained ever clear, were to be kept at an arm's length till the right time which he himself would duly declare. His children had to obey this.

In his quest for Miss Pheromone's love, Bob had a number of possibilities to mull over. One was the idea of asking to use a friend's personal hut for an intimate encounter with Miss Pheromone. He had no personal hut. His father had decided that having one would only be a source of temptation and so it was to be avoided.

Bob dropped this particular idea. The bush or maize plantation would be a better bet, for then only he and the girl herself would be aware of their deeds. Involving an extra party, however trustworthy, was a potential source of leakage to his father. He was pragmatic enough to understand that one never could block others' mouths if they already possessed the information. The bearers of the secret would let it out sequentially. With a hand partially blocking the gossipy mouth, the first one would warn the second against telling the secret to anyone else.

The second one later would warn the third in the same vein, adding that he had been warned but was sharing the secret only because he trusted the third person to be a strict keeper of secrets. Even more creative warnings would be created while the whole thing spread till it got to hit scandalous proportions.

Grabbing her by force was another of the plans he entertained. He dropped this too, and immediately. The competition may have been stiff but this measure was extreme apart from the fact that carrying it out successfully would certainly require the help of a different party.

Bob's mind moved on to yet another mechanism. It had been among the most hotly discussed subjects at the shade under the able facilitation of Owiti the chairman. It was the scientific approach to seduction. Bob gave a great deal of thought to the scientific approach to love. Bush chemistry, a contributor had said with conviction, worked wonders with the girls. For about ten minutes the contributor had held everyone's attention outlining the process of applying the use of charm on a girl whom your heart desired but was playing hard-to-get.

Oh, even this never quite convinced him as appropriate. It obviously would need teamwork. Once a secret left your heart even to a medicine man, people like his dad certainly would get wind of it.

There were no foolproof ideas coming to his mind. He felt somewhat frustrated, defeated. However, he consoled himself that he had the will and so there had to be a way, a way for him to Miss Pheromone's heart.

Chapter 5

No doubt, Andrea was a very bright person. Of all Miss Pheromone's suitors, he appealed to her specially. It was his linguistic acumen. His eloquence was unmatched. He had this unique capacity to use language finely in constructing powerful, logical arguments. This capacity placed him in a class of his own.

Miss Pheromone enjoyed every single minute of Andrea's company. Without saying it, she admired his speech. She didn't display this too openly; but it was unmistakable in her nearly constant smile while Andrea spoke, even nodding at this point or the other when Andrea unleashed a particularly pleasant expression.

The two were now in Miss Pheromone's grandmother's living room, this popular venue since the city girl came here. As it were, it was Andrea's day. He was having quality time with the village's most popular visitor ever.

A lot of pleasant things were said. A smile would be permanently planted upon Miss Pheromone's face as Andrea delivered a beautifully worded account of certain happenings in the locality. From him, Miss Pheromone learnt that she had to refrain from eating even fruits publicly as it was a fact that by just being looked at she could develop an alimentary complication. Radiations of certain dangerous characteristics, Andrew explained, emanated from the eyes of certain people if they looked fixedly at you while you ate. The radiations had high penetrative power and would reach the internal body part that such an evil individual wished to harm.

"Only certain people's eyes can produce that effect?" Miss Pheromone probed, an expression of amazement now replacing the smile that had been on her face.

"That's right. One is born with that power. On rare occasions it can be induced in a dark ritual; but even then, a candidate without any trace of that innate potential cannot be successful."

"Let me look at you fixedly to see if I have a trace of that innate potential," said Miss Pheromone jokingly.

"Hey, it's not a laughing matter," cautioned Andrea, smiling.

"Actually I am very serious. Let me put it this way: can I have myself tested – just in case I have that dangerous... thing?" said Miss Pheromone.

"Never trouble trouble till trouble troubles you, you know," said Andrea coolly and with finality.

Miss Pheromone had Andrew explain many other things. She hung on to his every word. Her grandmother entered the house and went on to an inner room, never saying a word to the two. How could she interfere with such deep concentration on the part of her listening granddaughter and the captivating speech from the young man? Within no time at all she emerged from that inner room bearing a small pail containing flour. Andrea stopped to grant the old lady attention. He offered her hearty greetings, both he and Miss

Pheromone laughing off their having been so engrossed in their conversation. Miss Pheromone's grandmother enthusiastically urged the two to go on with their great conversation, adding that lunch for them would be ready in just a little while. She proceeded to the kitchen.

After they had had lunch Andrea begged to leave, noting that he could not believe half the day was already gone. He thanked Miss Pheromone for the good time they had had together. She replied that pleasure was all hers. She saw off her visitor.

Now alone on his way to his place, Andrew reflected on the time he had spent with Miss Pheromone. He criticized himself for not having divulged the contents of his heart all that while. True he and Miss Pheromone had had a good time but he had failed as a man. A man needed to make moves, especially if a moment was as opportune as this had been, he thought. A whole half of a day with the most beautiful girl in the world, whom many other men sought to love, and nothing happens which is worth reporting to friends!

Chapter 6

Apidi never talked much. None ever could tell for sure whatever he was up to at any given time. He had come to be known as Apidi the silent killer. His deeply set eyes and the tendency to walk, looking onto the ground most of the time, only served to intensify the enigma that was part and parcel of his personality. Now, he, too, was in the race to Miss Pheromone's heart.

One of the strong points he could count on was his neatness. Apidi was clean at all times. His body and clothes sparkled. At his place, there was only some heavy iron box heated with either charcoal or burnt cobs of maize. Burnt tree barks also did well, particularly thick ones. When he used it to press his clothes, the outcome was amazing. The two parallel lines he loved to press onto his shirt down either breast made the villagers say that his shirt could cut up a housefly that dared to land upon it.

However, he hardly needed this iron box to look his neatest every dawning day. Apidi folded his shirts and trousers very neatly, using his palms to straighten up every crease as much as this could have them. He then placed these underneath the mattress. As he slept, his weight performed miracles on the clothes. It was a truly effective, stress-free, as well as time-saving method.

His teeth were easily the cleanest in the entire village. They were white, even and very strong. The chewing stick was his trick. He said the juice in the stick was medicinal, apart from the fact that it lent the mouth its pleasant fresh smell that lasted longer in the mouth than toothpastes did. Apart from cleaning them, Apidi ensured the health of his teeth by crushing tough foodstuffs such as raw cassava and roasted dry maize. He loved chewing sugarcane too.

Nonetheless, Apidi was yet to find a working formula when it came to approaching and sustaining a meaningful conversation with a girl. For this reason he had been taking very seriously some of those discussions that Owiti led at the big shade. Much had been discussed and with much enthusiasm: how to call a girl to you, how to start and sustain a meaningful conversation with her, how to tell her that you love her, how to invite her to your place for a visit, how to get a shy girl talking, how to handle a girl who is hostile towards your advances and so on. Still Apidi did not feel confident enough to apply such skills practically. Make no mistake though; he was no duffer. Actually, he did very well with those very close to him, chatting enthusiastically and even narrating accounts of pleasant or unpleasant personal experiences. Occasionally, he would let out a thunderous whoop, following it with some word of exclamation – sometimes a truly cheeky one. In a group, or with a stranger or more, however, he preferred to let others dominate everything.

Apidi once asked Andrea what exactly it was that one needed to say with a girl for so long. Did it not require about three minutes, or so, to tell a girl your name, maybe the village you came from, your school and class, and then tell her that you liked her and wanted her to be your friend?

Andrea had responded that that was basically what one needed to do; before adding an annoying 'however'. What Andrea had wanted Apidi to note, in spite of the correct formula he had outlined, was that talking to a girl was actually an art rather that some simple formula to be applied mechanically.

"Andrea, you are one of those who spoil girls, I realize," Apidi had interjected, cutting Andrea short. He was not coming to like the direction Andrea's explanation was taking. It would only have gone on to make him feel the more inadequate about his abilities. They would have done better to have switched to a topic they both could handle with ease and as equals rather than one creating difficult rules and trying to lecture the other on the same.

Now, concerning this competitive race towards Miss Pheromone's heart, in particular, what exactly did it take? Apidi wondered to himself. Would he need Andrea's little lessons which he had dismissed?

He would definitely find his way there; it was not for nothing that he was a man. A real man went out there and conquered whatever his heart desired, using whatever methods. The end always justified the means.

Unknown to Apidi, this same Andrea whom he thought he would do well to consult was experiencing his own personal crisis of confidence. It was one thing to be a good speaker and quite another to convince a girl to love you. This, exactly, is what Andrea told him this evening at Andrea's place, where he had gone for a consultation session with the master of communication affairs.

Apidi did not believe Andrea's easy admission as to difficulty in speaking to and convincing a girl to love you. He told himself that everyone required some time alone, at least at times.

Andrea determined that his approach to matters of the heart was the way to go; that one first established a basis for love, not just proposing it when a girl yet had no idea what to love about you. In view of this, he concluded to himself, he had actually not failed earlier in the day when he had been with Miss Pheromone all that time without declaring his love for her. This conclusion gave Andrea fresh energy. He decided to prepare for a further meeting with Miss Pheromone, during which he would present himself in a manner that would be consistent with the first impression she had had of him. He could not disown himself. Miss Pheromone just had to understand that he was a man who valued personal style, and his was an orderly and cultured self-presentation before others. His interaction with anyone had to show him for who he truly was, you know, what made him tick. He could not adopt anything superficial for the sake of whatever convenience he might be in need of.

Thus Andrea settled at his table, wearing a very serious face. He called in his little sister, whom he saw through the window passing by, and instructed her that he would require that his share of food be brought to him right there in his personal hut that evening, as he sought to concentrate on doing and completing something very important.

Andrea had gathered that Miss Pheromone was very well read. He might have done well in explaining to her certain interesting aspects of rural life but what if it came to displaying knowledge gained from books – which was, of course, much more serious? Would he do as well? He needed to be ready, very ready and prepared to do his very best when he next met Miss Pheromone. Once this was well done, making a proposal of love would be a small and easy matter, Andrea reckoned.

His earlier engagement with Miss Pheromone now stood him in good stead as he went through this process of personal preparation. He had a very good idea of the lines along which he needed to polish his mind, for the sake of an even more meaningful encounter with Miss Pheromone.

Miss Pheromone loved novels. He too loved novels and had, upon the reed-made shelf on the wall of his earthen hut, such copies as *My Life In Crime*, *Judy the Nun*, *Across the Bridge*, *Kill Me Quick* and some others. Their pages were yellow with age. The covers were no longer in place. Yet for others, quite a number of pages were torn, either in part or completely. But that never really mattered. He had enjoyed reading each of them.

He perused each of these books of his, reminding himself inside his head the names of the characters and the basic storyline of each. It always embarrassed him to talk to someone about a scene but referring to a book that had nothing to do with such a scene. Mentioning a character not found in the book you were discussing was another thing that he hated finding himself doing; not to forget assigning a book to the wrong author.

However, what Andrea dreaded most was being clueless about a book that a friend expected him to have read several times over. One always sounded like a very big fool just agreeing with the other person as they recounted the story events, to the extent that they became bored of narrating the story when they had wished to enjoy an informed, critical and intelligent discussion. Andrea patted himself on the chest, thanking his long established reading culture. Clearly, he said to himself, a book read is a saving made.

Having had his supper, which had been delivered here by his little sister, Andrea went on with the important task of preparing to meet Miss Pheromone. He now flicked through the pages of his huge compilation of hip hop lyrics and celebrity gossip. He had made such cuttings from newspapers. A few times he had run into trouble with his big brother, whose newspapers he cut thinking that once one was a day old, it became fit only for packing doughnuts or things like that. He had once responded to his brother's reprimand, saying that the newspapers which he cut were 'history'. His brother had asked him if he did not study history at school be he should mention it in such negative light. But his persuasive tongue had his otherwise irked brother still discussing the same annoying subject to the point where he told Andrea to cut out only the page containing lyrics and none other, strictly. Andrea, of course, had been okay with that.

Andrea fell asleep holding a magazine on men and cars. This one would actually give him power over Miss Pheromone; such that she would listen to him talk of the various car models: the capacity of their engines, the superiority of the gears of one over those of the other, their shapes, the countries and companies that manufactured them, their upper speed limits, their durability, their effectiveness on this or that kind of terrain, their prices in various world currencies, and all that. Here, Miss Pheromone would contribute only by asking Andrea questions, and not on equal terms as would be the case when they would be discussing books and celebrity gossip. So, even the sleep that had now stolen him knew that he was good to go.

Chapter 7

So it was now an established fact that Onyiego was never a man to be deterred by personal limitations. He preferred to focus on what he had to offer and not what he was unable to offer. Where his language was not polished, he had a lot of enthusiasm for life. As was very clear the time he was in Miss Pheromone's company, if ever there was something to laugh about, he did this heartily. If there was need to defend someone or something, whether verbally or physically, he could be counted on to do very well.

Miss Pheromone was to hugely benefit from Onyiego's willingness to be at her service. One evening, he actually took a water pot off Miss Pheromone's head and placed it on his own. Side by side they walked up to her grandmother's place. Of course, on their way, it was Miss Pheromone and her cousins who kept up the conversational fire burning, though Onyiego also tried his best to appear to be following whatever was being said. He had laughed, wondered aloud, and asked a few third-rate questions. As it were, it was always a good feeling to know that you tried your best. Indeed, Onyiego always tried his best.

The competition always does not take it kindly to notice that you are making headway. Onyiego's act was witnessed by the three other serious contenders. Why was Onyiego trying too much just to impress? Besides, were there no more manly ways to impress a girl than to bear a pot on the head? Surely, he was bringing great shame to all the village young men, went the popular feeling. He had to be censured at the big shade the following evening.

Meanwhile, Andrea had also pulled a new one to stay ahead of the competition. From an earlier conversation with Miss Pheromone, he had come to realize that there were books he had and had read that she neither had nor had read. It was actually the case with Andrea himself, only that Miss Pheromone had packed just two novels on this visit.

Andrea, therefore, had a ready excuse to visit Miss Pheromone time and again. Her grandmother at one time had noted to her that that boy of hers really knew the language of the white man, speaking it very fast.

Needless to say, this was a nod of approval; and when later Miss Pheromone had related it to Andrea, he had felt very good about himself and got even more encouraged to visit. It was never a small thing that the grandmother of your girl should think well of you and your abilities.

Apidi was not to be left behind either. Miss Pheromone's grandma was now assured of tilapia every evening. Apidi delivered this in person, fresh from the lake. He was an expert at fishing with the hook.

When his coming bearing this generous gift became perfectly predictable, Grandma started to make millet porridge, sweetened very much. Apidi would lay the fish upon Grandma's rack and Grandma would hand him a huge calabash of this sweet porridge. He could always guess the taste before bringing the calabash to meet his lips; therefore, he would swallow quite some amount of saliva as a prelude to the drinking itself. He sat and enjoyed his porridge, conversing in somewhat hushed tones with Grandma. Grandma would at one point or another burst out in laughter. What these two found so interesting remained everyone's guess though.

Grandma would later make one of those somewhat enigmatic remarks of hers. She now said to her granddaughter that she should live with her there permanently. That way, she would continue to eat tilapia without having to buy it. Miss Pheromone again just laughed, amidst which she remarked that Grandma was funny.

Bob was unfortunate though. Genuine as his love might have been, if his presence was so rare, who would go seeking him out to come and demonstrate his love? If you needed something, you needed to appear to be in needed of it. After all, they say, out of sight, out of mind! Had he lost interest? Or was he suffering from overconfidence? Overconfidence was especially well known as one of the major reasons men lost those they wanted for sweethearts.

These questions about Bob had crossed Miss Pheromone's mind when she woke up one morning. Bob was a very handsome boy; tall and dark too. His voice was pleasant: it made a girl feel really secure and loved.

Then she remembered the graphic description Bob had presented to her concerning his own father. It was a picture of hell itself, this place with which he threatened believers in almost every one of his passionately delivered sermons. The lovely guy was in bondage in the name of his father's religious fanaticism. She may have to do something to break those chains off Bob's hand, Miss Pheromone thought.

Bob was capable of life; you readily saw this, first thing when you met him. This was precisely what Miss Pheromone had noticed the day Bob had walked towards her spotting a bit of a bounce. He had shaken her hand confidently, looking into her eyes like a gentleman.

She would hatch a salvation plan, implement it, and thus give Bob the joy of life. He deserved it; everybody deserved it. In this world, reasoned Miss Pheromone, one had just one life and one owed it to oneself to be happy. It was not right that one man should place another in an environment of constant worry about where to go and where not to go; who to associate with and who not to associate with; what to think and what not to think; what to read and what not to read; what to listen to and what not to listen to; and all. It was prison; and of a very, very bad kind.

Chapter 8

Now, when a child cries for a razor, give it to him, the people of Hera village had always said. Miss Pheromone never saw why she should deny these men what they wanted. She would serve all the four men in equal measure. Each had worked so hard after his own unique manner, and therefore deserved appreciation. In any case, she determined, it was for her that they had gone the lengths they had.

Miss Pheromone had handled a variety of men, even simultaneously. She knew how to appeal to men: she knew what to say to a man, she knew how to drive a man expertly up to his greatest point of weakness. And it was at such a point that she would extract out of the very depths of that man's heart whatever she might have wanted to. She had done it with the men in town; these village ones would indeed come to regard her as the goddess of love herself.

Andrea would be the first to get his share of Miss Pheromone's warmth. She wrote him a letter. He felt weak in the knees, elbows and waist upon reading it. Such was the seductive power of that letter that Andrea admitted to himself that he was actually overwhelmed.

She had noted that she desired to discover Andrea in the most wholesome manner possible; to know what made him tick. He, on his part, needed to cause her to realize herself to the greatest depths, even re-invent her. This would happen when they next met.

This message had been passed across in the kind of English that Andrea would certainly appreciate forever. The general attitude of the letter had made it clear that its author regarded Andrea's language as what had him stand head and shoulder above all the rest.

When she and Andrea finally met, at her grandma's place, there was not to be even a second lost. A man, Miss Pheromone pointed out to Andrea, needed one thing: the woman.

And if ever words were necessary, then to her it was, absolutely, the reason the two of them had written each other the deepest of things any two souls could ever exchange. It was, really, rather insensitive taking much of a man's time in the hard-to-get kind of games.

Andrea had no words. He had needed these in their numerous conversation sessions there before. This, certainly, was not one such session. He used protection, which she had made available, but with some difficulty in the process. He never paid attention to what the matter might have been.

As Miss Pheromone saw him off, she praised his performance; likening it to his very command of language. Indeed, she added, she felt re-invented and had discovered that Andrea's strength was real and intrinsic.

Andrea never said much all that while, feeling less free than he would actually be when he would sit in the privacy of his hut to pen his appreciation of Miss Pheromone and what she had given him.

If he kept it all secret, Miss Pheromone told him, he may stand another chance; but he had to note that Miss Pheromone could take anything lightly but not her name being part of some braggadocio at some stupid gathering under some tree, in proof of how manly someone was. Here, Miss Pheromone was playing upon Andrea's sense of personal dignity, a characteristic that not only married well with his speech but had also come to define his very personality. Andrea, Miss Pheromone had come to gather, would go any length to guard his reputation. Indeed, he would obey this queen whose word, he noted gently as he closed the gate behind him, was his command. He had better things to do than to shoot himself in the foot, he had added colourfully and meaningfully. Indeed, none but Andrea was capable of saying such expensive things.

Chapter 9

Onyiego resorted to traditional love charm as the sure way for him to win Miss Pheromone. All his faith, all his confidence, was now in nothing but the love portion he had sought from a neighbouring village.

Because the other suitors always made a point of informing on the competition, of course with a view to discrediting them, Miss Pheromone always knew each one's scheme beforehand. She was always ahead of them even as each made what he thought of as a watertight romantic game plan. Indeed she was perfectly aware of Onyiego's endeavour in seeking traditional medicine with which to charm his way into her heart, and the fact that he had managed to come by the same.

So, when Onyiego appeared so as to implement the instructions of the love doctor, Miss Pheromone staged an act. She kissed him upon the lips, the very first time anyone had done that to Onyiego. He took this in stride, aware that he had just shaken her hand with the love powder rubbed onto his palms. This kiss had to be evidence of nothing but the effectiveness of the medicine, he firmly convinced himself. The actress played on.

He had been told, as well, to be sure that the target would follow him to wherever he wished. He had wished that Miss Pheromone should follow him to his personal hut. This, in any case, was where he had days on end spent a lot of thought upon this girl, and not to mention his having stayed up nearly all night earlier on, thinking of why the likes of Apidi, Bob, and the rest wanted the very girl he did. He had gone on empty stomach then; neither had he cared for breakfast the morning that followed, till he had personally delivered his love letter to her.

Now in bed with Onyiego, Miss Pheromone got him to his weakest point; at which point she dug expertly deep down Onyiego's heart of hearts. Onyiego came to reveal to Miss Pheromone that his greatest difficulty on earth was summoning the courage to tell a girl that he loved her. This, he added, was not a matter of ordinary shyness. There was this nickname Bure. Everyone used it on him. It had been derived from the local equivalent of the word 'worthless'. This was what his dad had always called him, as far as he could remember, never his name 'Onyiego'. Everybody else knew him as Onyiego Bure. The man was not really his father, and thus he had chosen to plant this fact deep inside Onyiego's heart through that sort of reference.

At this point of Onyiego's greatest vulnerability, Miss Pheromone kissed him on the lips and, looking straight into his eyes, said to him that no more did he have to dread 'disclosure'.

She had said this matter-of-factly, classifying Onyiego's psychological difficulty using that powerful term 'disclosure'. He now believed she was a goddess! She had solutions. He would hold onto her with two hands. Anything she would ask for, that would he meet without any qualms. No wonder, thought Onyiego, he had felt so helpless the day he had been borne shoulder-high from the foot of the euphorbia tree. No wonder he had sobbed uncontrollably, even rolled on the ground like an animal.

"I am your true and only love," Miss Pheromone went on, now with her hands upon the shoulders of Onyiego, so that his face was consumed in her awesome gaze. "You will marry me, if that's what your heart desires; and I know it is. I would not have opened up to you this much if I did not feel that you are the one who was made for me," she went on in a masterfully seductive voice, now rendering Onyiego completely weak in the joints. He felt as if she had killed him with love.

Now, that was what it took to secure Onyiego's solemn undertaking that he would not so much as allude to this instance of intimacy. When Miss Pheromone sought his undertaking in his actual words, his response was a miracle for a man of his communication ability. He had said that he would not choose to lose such a golden soul-mate who had come to solve the most fundamental of his problems: love.

Chapter 10

Apidi, who had been planning to waylay Miss Pheromone and drag her into the bush, had his plan side-stepped when he received word that Miss Pheromone wished to meet him in his personal hut. Bob had been the informer this time round.

Apidi's plan had been based upon his own conclusion that he never could come to be in control even when he had done well to secure Miss Pheromone's attention. To him, she seemed to take advantage of his difficulty with words, and thus ending up dominating over him so much that he felt totally emasculated at the end of the encounter.

A girl, in Apidi's estimation, even if she was very great, needed to let the man be in control. Besides, men not quick with words, such as was the case with him, needed to be understood to be men of action! Yet Miss Pheromone's attitude clearly indicated that she had judged him as incapable of anything. This was not good at all.

Anyway, Miss Pheromone's charm offensive inside his own hut had Apidi quickly and completely revise his view of this girl. He came to realize that she understood the nature of men, and of life itself, as a matter of fact.

When Apidi had been led to and safely kept at his weakest point, he had revealed to Miss Pheromone that his aggressive tendencies were not only in response to his inarticulate nature but were also a cover-up for his discomfort with his deeply set eyes about which everybody made fun.

Likewise, Apidi was effectively assured that he and his personal fears were perfectly safe with this goddess, inside her warm and understanding heart. But most important, he now had been set absolutely free, owing to the fact that he needed not disclose his vulnerability to anyone else for she was all in all. Men, she informed him, never liked having to make such disclosures as he had today made to her. It bruised their ego a great deal. Thus, what he had done, in sharing with her such details, meant that an unbreakable bond had been established between them forever. She would love him unconditionally.

With that assurance, Apidi felt on top of the world. He felt that she should not leave his presence; not now, not any other time. It was dawning on him that love was the most powerful thing on earth.

Miss Pheromone had to leave as it was getting dark. Apidi offered to escort her to her place, but she reminded him that everything needed to be kept at a very low profile lest idle tongues should spoil their love even before it began to blossom.

He, as well, was to undertake that he would not blab; and Apidi was emphatic that never would he betray himself, much less so in such a stupid manner as going about bragging that he had made love to Miss Pheromone.

Chapter 11

So much for the holiday! Miss Pheromone now had to return to the city. She was well over half-way through with high school. She had maintained a good record of performance at school.

To a lot of people this fact would be another of the wonders of Miss Pheromone's life. Such beautiful and highly pampered girls, even if basically smart, were assumed to have a negligent approach to even important things, including classwork. The world revolved around them, everyone naturally granting them attention, and in excess. They thus did not have to fight for anything. As a matter of fact it was for others to fight over them. Miss Pheromone, however, clearly had places to go via the academic highway. She had work to do to get to that highway. There would always be time for Hera village once important things were duly attended to and thoroughly taken care of.

Now, round about the time Miss Pheromone left for the city, Bob disappeared from home and the village. This was strange.

His father almost went mad. He cursed the Devil for stealing his child and complained to God as to why bad things were happening to him – of all people! Was he serving God in vain?

Bob arrived in the city. All was new to him, this being his first time ever here. All was fast.

Miss Pheromone showed him into a waiting taxi. Bob took the seat behind the driver. She negotiated the fare and then got herself into the taxi, sitting next to Bob.

"The city is not going to disappoint you," she said to Bob.

"I'm sure I'll love it," said Bob, his gaze fixed right in front.

The driver manoeuvred his way out of the packed street and onto the main avenue. He would deliver these two to a city estate not very far from the central business district. It was in that estate that Bob was to begin life in the city.

Miss Pheromone was a genius. How she had made these arrangements while in the village, Bob could not tell. All she had let him know three days to the end of her holiday visit in Hera was that he would start life in the city in a cheap single room, and that it would be upon him to take advantage of city opportunities to graduate from there to a better house and estate. Bob had never been able to conceal the fact that he felt scared about having to leave the security of his father's home to try to survive all on his own among total strangers in a faraway city. Miss Pheromone had read his psychology and rebuked him for behaving like some scared little girl. She had moved to reassure Bob that his being scared of the city was normal especially given that not one bit of his life had been lived outside Hera; but that a decision should never be made on the basis of fear, fear of nothing but living among fellow human beings struggling through life just as everyone else was doing. She had added that if Bob could put up with the kind of life he was living, and was bound to continue living at home, then he needed not leave for the city. Upon the sound of this, Bob had said that his mind was already made up; he was leaving home.

Bob had disguised himself as a Muslim girl wearing a full dress, the face completely veiled. Thus dressed, he had boarded an early morning bus to the city. According to their arrangement, Miss Pheromone would leave the village in broad daylight so that the villagers get to see her leave just as they had seen her arrive there.

Upon reaching the city, Bob would stay put at the bus station till Miss Pheromone got there and found him.

And now here they were in this single room. She had spoken on the phone with the lady who owned it, and agreed with her that she would deliver the rent for the first month on the spot when she brought the new tenant. This was an aunt to her best friend at school.

Miss Pheromone left Bob with the words, "Find something to do, anything. The city will not disappoint you. Live life."

So Bob settled in the room, Miss Pheromone's last words ringing acutely in his mind. He had chosen to come to the city; he had to get something to do – anything that would ensure that he at least never starved in this little space that was his abode. He was determined to make it. He was not the first to have come to the city to begin life from zero.

If his father offered people salvation, mused Bob, here was a superior savior, who set the heart free and absolutely so. Miss Pheromone had given him life itself. She had shown him so practically how useless it was to stay in such lifelessness as the bondage in which he lived within his father's delusional perspectives on life, as well as the narrow and limiting village life.

Chapter 12

Bob began life in the city from scratch, as it were. He had quit secondary school a year to completion. Now without a secondary school certificate, he had little option but to settle for anything that would enable him to pay rent for some rather humble house.

He took up a job as a waiter at a downtown restaurant. Here, they offered chips and chicken. The city people loved these a lot, and either sat in there and ate or asked that the food be packed for them to carry away. In the latter case, Bob and fellow waiters would be instructed by a customer in the simple words 'take-away'.

Bob would then open the grill inside which the chicken rotated slowly, draw out one, cut it up into pieces convenient for packing, place these pieces in a transparent polythene material, wrap the same with a newspaper leaf and finally place all this in yet another transparent polythene material and give it to the esteemed customer to 'take away'. The waiters had always been urged to do all this wearing the most pleasant faces they could afford.

In this job, he would be paid two thousand shillings at the end of the month, and daily bonuses depending upon the daily profit margin. He lived with a workmate of his both for company and to split up the cost of rent between them. They did very well, by their own standards, mostly taking time to enjoy the days of their youth in the city.

Having waited on customers for about three months, Bob's life was now taking a new turn. This was occasioned by a discovery he made about himself upon prompting by his fellow waiter and housemate, who thought that Bob could rap and sing very well. Bob's voice, he had said, had this pleasantly deep and melodious quality. Bob could make real money out of it, for some of those who were already driving flashy cars there in the city had such raspy voices, anyway.

Bob revealed to his colleague that he and family did sing in the church choir, hence the ease with which he sang well. He added, however, that never had he imagined himself doing secular music; it just never crossed his mind.

Clearly, he was yet under the powerful influence of his father's prescribed way of life, which required that he and his entire family saw no evil, heard no evil and touched no evil.

Bob amazed himself by the speed at which he was loosening up for the city life. The numerous shows he attended, again mostly at the prompting of his friend, had worked through him within no time.

Soon Bob could say a few lines of rap after the manner of the artistes whom he watched. In the house, he would spot a bandana; and in his sagging jeans trousers, tight t-shirt and sport shoes, he was a celebrity in his own right. A bouncy walking style, a curving of the arms with fingers spread apart when speaking, a mixture of English and Swahili; this bespoke one thing: Bob was now an artiste wannabe and an artiste he would be.

Within no time at all, Bob was now in the category of an up-coming musician. When Miss Pheromone visited his new rental, she was genuinely happy for him. She was pleasantly surprised that Bob now rapped and sang rhythm and blues. She reminded him of his former life and alerted him of this absolute transformation.

In such situations, Miss Pheromone could be depended upon to do what she did best: make the victim of her charm ever more to believe in her powers and no one else's. Now she sought to heap credit upon herself for Bob's upward mobility, and at the same time appeal to his desire to climb higher and higher up the ladder of success.

Thus, now playing the role of a motivational speaker, she was taking this golden and well-timed opportunity to share with Bob a bit on this thing called success. She entitled her sharing: 'How to Become Rich in One Hundred Days.'

She told Bob to observe six things strictly: follow your heart; produce great quality of what you have to offer; produce great quantity of what you have to offer; believe that no one is better than you; ignore detractors; act and think as though you already are what you want to become; and have only one girlfriend.

Amazing! Miss Pheromone was telling Bob the very things he wanted to hear. He had wanted her to carry on speaking; for, whatever she said was very good. However, she had to get back to her father's place before seven o'clock, the evening time past which she would have to contend with one of those rare but powerful lectures her father would give her for such disobedience. This was the last thing she would ever wish for. A doting father Mathew Pheromone may have been but disobedience he never took lightly.

That said, Miss Pheromone hugged Bob tightly, telling him that she loved him very much and would visit him as frequently as was convenient for both of them, to give him love even more creatively than she had done today. She got to her father's place in time.

Chapter 13

Bob's music hit television screens. Only his own voice rivaled his looks. His music bespoke pure talent. His stage name stuck onto every lip. Both the young and the young at heart adored him. To them, he was Bobbystar.

Fans drooled over Bob, literally. They wanted him – you know, to greet them, to sign on their autograph books, to show them the cheekiest, most suggestive of dance moves upon the stage, and all that. And he gave them what they wanted, always.

Bobbystar's debut single propelled him to instant fame. The song topped popular entertainment charts. Fans sang along wherever and whenever they heard 'My Baby', not only recalling it word for word but also trying, as much as each one's degree of musical giftedness allowed, to hit the high notes and do the voice shaking at the climactic portions of that tantalizing and sizzling love song. The owner outdid them only slightly. The next thing was that everyone now wanted to know more about the girl to whom Bobbystar directed such hot romantic passion in the video. Was there something going on for real?

Now, to be sure, such questions always emanated from some point; they never were just out of the blue. Everybody wanted to know this same thing: radio and television entertainment show hosts, fans during the phone-in sessions, contributors in newspaper entertainment columns and magazine articles, just everyone.

Now someone was at the door, knocking. It was Miss Pheromone. This was yet another of her frequent visits here. Bob felt glad. He would seek her advice as to how to go about handling the question from the public. He opened the door and ushered her in with a hug.

Having taken a seat, Miss Pheromone called Bob's name contemplatively. She told him that she was doing a great deal of souls-searching as to what to do with her life. She said she was almost arriving at a decision but that the decision certainly would sharply clash with her father's. Once she would reach a conclusion, that would be the way to go, as it would be the sure way for her to live a happy life.

"What, to you, is happiness?" posed Bob.

"Happiness is what I decide it is."

"Just anything one decides?"

"Listen, Bob. I want us to understand happiness as the emotion that it is, not as whatever we have already fixed in our imagination."

"All right."

"Bob, happiness is an emotion just as anxiety, worry or anger is. Needless to say, in life we cannot avoid feeling anxious, worried or angry, as these are facts of life. Nonetheless we do often decide what we are not going to allow to worry us or to get us angry. To be sure, many things that we listen to or witness have the potential to annoy or even enrage us. Fortunately, we do make a conscious choice to ignore a great proportion of such so that in their place we have positive emotions, such as the good feeling we have when sharing laughter. That aside, we deem certain things amusing yet such may never be any of that at all. Our getting amused at a certain thing is a result of interplay among many different factors within or around us.

Let me point out to you, as well, that people will discover an outstanding thing about themselves and decide to make it the basis of their happiness."

"Which is all right – I suppose. Beautiful people should want the whole world to behold that beauty – whether on glamourous magazine covers, on the screen, on billboards, on the internet, wherever."

"If that is their best point of strength then it is all right."

"I am not sure I understand you."

"People choose. I must carefully and keenly consider all my points of strength. Indeed if possible I should get to test each of them just to find out how much happy it'd make me if I chose it at the expense of all the others."

"I think that in your case it would be best that you choose to be a model. Why do you deny magazines and screens that face?"

"Let me find this out from you, Bob. You do think that my looks are the greatest thing about me, don't you?"

"Well, that I cannot say. Perhaps I am yet to find out a few more things about you that may turn out to be greater about you than your looks are. Insofar as I can tell though, I hold that you'd be the finest model ever to have graced the catwalk anywhere in the world."

"People may enjoy looking at me – and I appreciate it, by the way. However, does anyone ever give thought to the idea that I personally enjoy something totally different from my looks?"

"Well, and to be very honest, I personally find you exceptionally intelligent. Talking to you, for instance, is always a great experience. The things you say, how you express them… This is one quality in you I would confidently describe as exceptional."

"I see. Thank you."

"However, in that particular regard you still would have to think of what exactly it is that you would do with that otherwise great ability in order for you to have something that the world practically appreciates.

Please, get me right, that 'something' certainly could be there. I do not rule it out. The point, however, is that beauty, such as what you have here, is a guarantee for fame and good life, you know."

"Why don't we carry on with this particular discussion next time. I wish I could stay longer."

"This would go into record as your shortest ever visit to my place."

"Actually, I was sent to town for this…"

"Looks to me like a chandelier."

"You guessed right. I just felt I should drop by to broach this matter of what I am to do with my life so you and I can handle it together."

"Oh, thanks a lot for dropping by. One thing that pleases me about that whole matter is that whatever it is you will settle upon will only yield greatness. You are a specially and beautifully talented person. Anyway let me not hold you any longer."

Bob, there's something I'd like you to discover about me, something that matters infinitely more than…Shall we do this next time?"

"Of course that is all right."

"See you."

"See you."

"Live life."

"I will."

Bob's mind returned to his earlier thoughts. He had always maintained in the interviews that the song in question simply had come out well following one of his fundamental principles in music practice: always produce great quality. It had simply been a determination to give his listeners the very best he could. It was not about him being in love.

Oh, the more he attempted to explain away the matter, the greater the attention it received. Spying ensued. Paparazzi hit the road.

So passionately did Bobbystar sing to that girl in the video that there had to be emotional attachment between him and that object of his affection in the wonderful song; and the attachment had to be at an advanced level.

Eventually, he gave in to the astounding persistence and admitted on air that that was actually his one and only girlfriend and that as soon as she finished school, he would marry her.

Little known to Bob was that this was a major blunder. Among the curious lot were a chain of boyfriends Miss Pheromone maintained. Such had been her expertise at multiple-dealing that only a few of the men ever came to know of each other's relationship with her.

Miss Pheromone's strongest power was her way with words. She had this seductive tone of voice that disarmed you instantly if ever there arose even a semblance of contention. You never even contemplated an argument with her.

When she was with a man, she made him feel so special that there never arose any possibility of suspicion. Having thus made a man feel that he was the best thing that ever happened to life and that he had no reason whatsoever to doubt her, she elicited out of that man an undertaking that he would never blab. She made it abundantly clear that she had problems with publicity and would cut ties as soon as she heard that people knew of the relationship. A man, of course, would but protect the bird in hand if the requirement only was: not talking about it.

Yet apart from that, she had this irresistible sense of sophistication; and a great brain to boot. The girl could lead someone on expertly. She played her love games smartly and it worked for her.

The games were deliberate. She would say that a beautiful, intelligent and hugely gifted girl such as she was had to have the very best of things life had to offer. She, for one, wondered why a girl should stick to one man, who, at the very best, could have but one truly strong point. She needed variety, which was the spice of life!

Therefore, at any given point in her life, said Miss Pheromone, she needed a 'strong pentagon of men'. One was her physical protector, and needed to be of powerful physic; another was her guide, and needed to be older and on a well-paying job; another one was her companion, and needed to be a schoolmate; the fourth one was her entertainer, and needed to be outgoing; and the fifth one was her true love, and needed to be good and innocent. Only then would she feel secure; and she always did until the above said media explosion.

It did not help matters that at the time Bob blabbed on air, Miss Pheromone had been watching the television with a newly acquired and the seventh of her boyfriends. She had, up to that, disclosure treated the matter of her appearance in the video with an absolute ease; even bragging that a beautiful girl would definitely be sought after to make a cameo appearance here and there, adding that more of such appearances were in the offing as a matter of fact.

So now Miss Pheromone had to watch over her shoulders lest she should succumb to the fury of a man seeking vengeance. She would from now on be very careful. She would be either at school or at home; no more of going out and all that. She would finish school and then marry Bob, the only husband material among the men she had known and dated so thoroughly. He was innocent and, most interesting, had proved obedient to her, heeding her advice that he should have only one girlfriend. He had remained faithful to her in spite of his being a musician. In interviews, he quoted her philosophies on success. This was amazing!

Chapter 14

It was a bit of a tussle between daughter and father as to whether she needed to marry as soon as she finished high school. To him, she needed a college education, which would enable her to settle down in some career. This, advised the father, would have her become basically independent in her life.

She had been very simple and straightforward with her father on this. She loved Bob more than anyone and anything. She had had men in her life; however, she had settled on Bob as the kind of man to marry. No other girl deserved Bob, and to delay would be to risk losing him.

Miss Pheromone told her father that she was marrying out of love and not out of need for a spouse.

She went further to offer that true love surpassed human understanding and, as such, could neither be debated nor directed.

Her father now remained silent as she said words, amid sobs, that did not have to remind him that he and her mother had divorced for having run out of love just four years into their marriage. She herself, she said, had done her homework well and found a goldmine of love; and nobody, not even her father, had any right to take this away from her. She added that she had done all he had wanted her to do as a student and was sure that the results of the examination she had just sat were going to please him and make him proud as a father.

Therefore, this was the time for her to do what would please her and make her proud as an individual soul.

Mathew Pheromone was not given to dictating to others; least of all on matters of fundamental choice. He had played his role as a father and ensured his girl stayed in school to completion. There was no doubt that she would pass her exams well and own an impressive certificate. He left the living room for his bedroom.

For some time it was silent tension in the Pheromone household. Father and daughter said little. The matter weighed heavily on both of them. Any decision on the matter would be profoundly life-changing.

When Mathew Pheromone let his daughter know that he had weighed the matter seriously and settled on supporting her decision, he made her very excited all of a sudden, after days of sulking. She rushed up to him, hugged him and said to him that he was the best father in the whole world.

And so Miss Pheromone went up to Bob's place. She felt that it was high time she told Bob what exactly she had decided to do with her life. And she told him, tears of love flowing freely down her cheeks, that all she wanted in life was to be his wife. She said that unless this happened, she could not be the model that Bob wished she should be or the many other things she herself planned to pursue in her life.

Bob took her in his arms. He said nothing. He wiped off her tears gently with his hand. He was witnessing a totally new thing about Miss Pheromone. All he had hitherto known was this self-confident girl who feared nothing in life. He was holding a tender, vulnerable person. Resting there in his arms, she gave him the feeling that he was a great protector even though in truth he still held that she was his protector in addition to being his saviour.

She disengaged from his arms and lowered herself onto the sofa. She motioned him to get seated by her side, which he did, expecting her to tell him something that obviously was weighing heavily in her heart.

"Bob, you have no idea how much you mean to me," she began, the words originating from somewhere very deep inside her.

Once she had thus spoken, her heart became light and it was then possible for her to use her normal conversational tone in the rest of their stay there at her fiancé's place.

Chapter 15

Miss Pheromone now knew she would have the fairytale wedding she had dreamt of since she was little. This was one event whose details had long been printed upon her mind; one step after another. Therefore, any thought that her father would not be walking her down the aisle to give her off to her groom would have been a potential source of some real trouble. If it would not have been suicidal, it would have had her go ahead and wed without his blessings. The latter case would have had her live the rest of her life in the bitterness that her father, for a reason that had nothing to do with her love and happiness, had spoilt her life. A proper wedding, to a girl, was life itself, Miss Pheromone held.

Arrangements would now be made cordially. She was ecstatic about it all. She would link her family with her now superstar boyfriend in the wedding preparations. A well-to-do father, and an artiste of Bobbystar's caliber, was all a girl needed to feel as if she were a princess upon her big day.

A top city designer was contracted to make a wedding dress in the order of that which had been worn by the Princess of Wales at her fairytale wedding. As for the ring, who would have known better than Bob did what it was that would please a woman?

The designing of the wedding cake, a five-tier one supported upon four three-tier ones; the matching attire of the bridesmaids, flower girls and page boys; the tuxedo suits and maroon bow ties of the groom and best man; the heavy media presence to capture the images of this celebrity event; and all that was now within Miss Pheromone's grasp, not any more a little girl's dream.

Bob's family had since come to terms with the fact that in life no one and nothing may hold down an individual who had made up their mind to pursue a given heartfelt cause. A religious family had produced a secular superstar. It was real and they had embraced it in the words 'God works in ways we mortals cannot comprehend.'

There was a heavier representation from Bob's family than from the Pheromones at the grand wedding. His mother was there too, so elegant in a royal blue silky dress and a graceful headgear, spotting a flower garland. His father was there in a shiny black suit. His siblings too were there. Arrangements had been made as well to have as many of the village members as was possible come up to the city, for Bob was their son of whom they were very proud, especially owing to his unrivaled musical prowess.

Bob was beside himself with joy. He had never experienced a better feeling than this; neither would he, he mused, holding hands with his best man. His bride was somewhere in the congregation and he was to find her.

Miss Pheromone was in her immaculate wedding gown. Her plump shoulders showed; and they were very smooth and soft to the eye. You felt like touching them. Her face was under the veil.

The garden wedding commenced at ten o'clock sharp that beautiful sunny morning. Guests had done very well to keep time. Most of them were the local artistes, who were also expected to stage performances here. Others were from the Ports Authority where Mathew Pheromone worked as a clearing and forwarding officer.

But it was the presence of a sea of fans that made this a wedding in a class of its own. When fans love you, they love you helplessly. The garden square compound hardly could take them all in. Some, therefore, watched it all from outside; some carrying each other in turns upon their shoulders so as to catch a glimpse. Others, however, just faithfully followed the voice of the commentator from the mounted speakers, believing that the commentator would be good enough to express in fitting words and tone of voice all that went on inside, so that at the end of it all, it would be as good as if they had seen it all personally.

The choir from Bob's home was great. Bob's father sang tenor there. He had always held that without song, not even a sermon ought to be delivered. As he stretched his vocal cords there today, veins of his neck showing prominently, heaven came down! Bob himself recalled his days on that side of life. It had been life as he had known it.

His sisters still sang there, today being the lead sopranos in their fresh youthful voices that now filled the air. The perfect blend of their rich high pitched tone sounded the word 'sweet' and all the voices joined in with 'Beulah Land' in the highly evocative song 'Sweet Beulah Land', they were now doing in the four voices.

For a moment, he thought to himself that singing for God had this unique way of elevating your heart to some sort of indescribable realm where there was this deeply satisfying glory. He wondered if everybody else here felt as he did.

Upon that solemn note, the bride and groom were now set to pronounce the marriage vows, Miss Pheromone reminding everyone of the Princess of Wales at her tell-tale wedding. The train of her white gown was almost as long as that of the said princess.

The groom was handsome, everybody knew this, always. No word, therefore, could do justice to his appearance today. You just fed your eyes on his looks and the happiness that was radiant upon the faces of the two of them.

The reverend in charge of Bob's father's church here in the city stepped forward. Cameramen never wanted to miss any of the emotions the bride and the groom would display at every point of what was the core of everything in a wedding. They wanted to record the kiss itself: how deep it would be, how long it would last, how comfortable or otherwise the couple would be doing this before thousands upon thousands of curious eyes.

Bob was first in repeating after the reverend the words of the marriage vows. His mellifluous voice was at its best. A bit of nervousness had made him take a deep breath just seconds before, which the reverend noticed; and he made pleasant fun out of it, much to the amusement of everyone.

The bride did her part as beautifully. They were declared husband and wife, the rest being warned in humble solemnity that they should not put asunder what God had put together.

Chapter 16

Mathew Pheromone was the owner of Pheromone Hotel, situated within the central business district of the capital city. A grand reception awaited his daughter and her superstar husband there.

It all looked to Mathew Pheromone as if it was a royal affair – this reception. You see, this was not just some three-star hotel in the city but, rather, his personal property; indeed, his castle, standing there so proudly. It was specially decorated today on the second floor where guests would be served.

Seated in his Peugeot 608 headed to Pheromone Hotel, he felt as though he were a king going to give his daughter the best treat in the world at his own palace. Perhaps the absence of his wife in his life added to the intensity with which he loved his daughter; and now he looked forward to delivering a befitting speech describing a man's joy at being successful and sufficiently happy despite odds.

The car bearing the parents of Bob followed closely, then that in which the newly-weds themselves were, and then a chain of several other cars taking the guests to the reception. Even strangers seemed happy for these people – whoever they were – who were so deep into the business of marriage. This was what was suggested by the faces of bystanders, pedestrians, those in personal cars and public service vehicles, and so on.

Twaap! Twaaap! Off went a pistol all of a sudden, the two bullets shattering the car window and finding their way to

Bob's comfortably seated self. The first one shattered his lower jaw and was stopped by Miss Pheromone's right shoulder, into which it was wholly lodged. The fatal one had got right into Bob's heart; and he was no more after a matter of minutes. She was rushed to a city hospital.

This was the work of thugs hired by one of Miss Pheromone's former boyfriends. They had accomplished their mission. The leisurely moving, balloon covered car bearing the newly-weds to the grand reception had been waylaid by these thugs at a forested section of the road, their spies having been doing their assigned roles with terrible accuracy through phone calls.

The thugs vanished into the forest, having added to the world record another item on the list of the shortest lasting marriages.

Those alive and uninjured had a grand confusion with which to deal in the best way they knew how. That was how life sometimes behaved: presenting to people a chapter so brief.

Chapter 17

Onyiego, Andrea and Apidi were doubly sad back in the village. They looked haggard even. First, they had lost a friend with whom they had involved in quite a few adventures, the quest for Miss Pheromone's heart having been but one of such. Secondly, they were now on those huge tablets of drugs called ARVs, the antiretroviral drugs. These would lengthen as much as possible the miserable lives they now led. They had, quite a while before, received the shock of their lives when the results of voluntary counselling and testing declared them HIV positive.

Miss Pheromone now received advanced medical attention, following her shooting. Ancillary tests on her blood had revealed that she was HIV positive. She would recover perfectly from the bullet wound and live positively with the virus.

Bob's family had taken the excruciating pain of loss in stride. They were ever a prayerful family, and prayers for fortitude came in handy at this difficult moment in their family's life. It was God, they firmly believed, who gave life; and when He decided to take it back to himself, His will needed to be accepted humbly. The villagers danced to Bob's own music at Bob's funeral that evening of his being laid to rest. They danced all night. Had he been alive, their hearts told them, he would be doing the same; what he had had only a short time to do, what he loved with his whole heart: music.

Death would not dampen their spirits. They knew that Bob lived on in his music and would go on and on, generations and generations to come. They knew, as well, that all things shall perish under the sky; that music, alone, shall live.

Days went by. Life went on; the sun rising and setting in its usual manner, perhaps aware, perhaps completely oblivious, of the events upon this earth whose surface its rays struck. The most painful of heartaches also had to give way, to allow newness to take its rightful place, just as fresh grass springs up in an earlier burnt area in the savanna.

Oftentimes, the three surviving victims of the adventure with Miss Pheromone would sit together at the home of any one of them just to talk; thereby encouraging one another. Their status by no means meant the end of life itself. No! They would continue to eat, converse, laugh, work, and so on, just as they had always done.

Andrea's command of language was by now legendary in Hera village and beyond. He continued leading conversations in whatever company he found himself. He had become a fitting, perhaps better, replacement of Owiti, who had left Hera for a faraway country in the south to go and work as a casual labourer at a newly discovered coal mine over there. He now described to the gathering at the big shade how once upon a time he saw a gold mine. He had rushed to extract the gold, this precious element of which every child of humanity dreamt whether while asleep at night or awake in broad daylight. He had used the method he understood to get inside the mine, and he made it in there. Therein, he saw that there were gold deposits, in great abundance. He would become the richest even among those who came with him into the mine. He dug the ore of gold and carried a lot of it out of the mine. He separated the glittering metal from everything else that was of no worth. However, when he presented his merchandise to the buyer, it was rejected, for it was not gold at all. He concluded that he had since wisened up and that he had made it his responsibility to remind everyone else that not all that glitters is gold.

Even Onyiego related this allegory to the lives of the three of them: he, Apidi and Andrea himself. Onyiego actually was nearly staggering with laughter where he was at the big shade with his village mates. Laughing about his situation had always been to him quite an effective coping mechanism in the face of harsh realities. It diffused stressful thoughts and feelings, as it were. His easy approach to life had also seen him take a girl with whom he now had a baby boy. Part of the counsel he and friends had got when they had gone for HIV testing was that they could still get a willing partner and have children; that there were chances that the virus did not infect the partner if the intercourse itself was conducted according to certain professional instructions. Infection of the baby during birth, they had been told, needed to be none of their worry for the experts knew how to prevent it from happening.

Apidi had come to like Andrea a lot. Only Andrea, in the whole wide world, gave him words and expressions. He had long taken up Andrea's wise saying that: cleanliness is next to godliness. Not only had Apidi personified this wisdom but he had also made the saying his own; everyone knew this was Apidi's wise saying. And Apidi would certainly carry on living it out in his personal bodily and sartorial care. He liked Onyiego too for his great attitude towards life. What he opted not to do was to take a bride for himself as Onyiego had. He would dedicate the rest of his life to seeking the knowledge of God and teaching it to others. At times he would feel really bad about certain basic personal limitations. He would blame the sort of schooling he had got for not having added much value to his life, for example by giving him knowledge of an international language. All he had was the Hera language, and so he could preach the word of God internationally as his heart now felt he should be doing.

Fate had bound these three together in a unique manner, and they were facing life just as it had been assigned unto them. They were not letting anything come between them and their happiness. They owed it to themselves to live life to its fullest. Andrea's love for words would be known even by generations to come. He had reasoned that a precious gift such as he had should be of use to others during and after his life. His novel manuscript, which he had entitled "Adventures with Miss Pheromone", had more than impressed a publishing agent who had come to Hera village all the way from the city upon getting word that there was a young man with such kind of work just lying in his personal hut. Indeed, Andrea's powerful expressions, which now rested in the pages of a book, would capture imaginations for generations. The book would be fine evidence that he lived. It would teach important lessons about life.

Chapter 18

Miss Pheromone was discharged from hospital two weeks after her admission there. The bullet wound was on course to healing. She had needed care related to coming to terms with both her marital loss and her new health status, and her father had ensured that she got exactly this.

She thanked her God that she was alive. It was not every day that one took time to do this; to be alive seemed a guarantee, even a right. Just certain things got one numbering one's days and feeling grateful for each breath drawn in then out.

She took stock of her young life. She formed a compact picture of it all in her mind; and took a close look at that picture.

She had failed herself and God; completely. She had it all: she was breathtakingly beautiful; she was intelligent; she was a gifted singer; and more. If her mother had left while she was still a little girl, did she not have a loving, even doting father? Yet what exactly was it that she could be proud of having done? Was it the chain of young men who hung around her all the time? And was this not the root cause of Bob's death, anyway?

She sobbed painfully, face cupped in her palms and buried between the knees. She had been cruel. She had led on many a man. She had badly used as many. She felt that she should die; and lay her body upon her bed that she may die.

Then an angel came unto her; a swift white angel that had outdone in flight a powerfully built and wide-winged black one. The white angel instructed her to get up right then and go to the convent, before the other angel reached her.

She woke up from her brief dream. She was panting and sweating. Her heart was beating very fast. She played back the dream in her mind. It was so vivid that there was no shadow of doubt in her mind as to what course the rest of her life should take.

She would dedicate the remaining part of her life, whether it would be long or short, to doing something that was above average; something she would, at the end of it all, feel proud to have done with her precious life.

Chapter 19

Miss Pheromone arrived at the Fountain Convent. She had carried no personal effects at all. She had only an extra dress forced into a small black polythene bag.

Her father had not been able to prevail upon her to abandon the idea of joining a convent, especially given her condition, which would soon become delicate. Besides, what did she know about a convent, anyway?

Oh, all his pleas had been to no avail. Here she now was, for real. She walked towards the office, having informed the guard at the gate that she was there to see the Mother Superior. On and on she walked, not really hurrying. The compound was silent and eerie.

From a distance she could see a nun in a brown habit scaling the stairs just where she herself was heading. Her steps began to be a little cowardly now. Doubts began to assail her. What exactly had she to tell the Mother Superior? Surely, she never could just allow her into the convent; some good reason had to be given, and tough questions asked and answered satisfactorily.

What, for instance, did she know about Fountain Convent or any other convent, for that matter? What did it take to gain admission there? How had she prepared for life at a convent? These and more questions crossed her mind, tangling in there with each other and with her determination to find a new life.

Miss Pheromone felt that she had made a grievous mistake leaving home. Her immediate worry, however, pressed her more: she was about to make a great fool out of herself before the Mother Superior, having come here but at an impulse, which she had fooled herself to be some white angel's message.

She went straight to the office of the Mother Superior, a greying old lady yet still so strong, so sharp in vision, hearing and mind. She had seen a thousand and one of such girls as Miss Pheromone here. They arrived here alone, and with moving stories as to why they had come to the convent. Whatever the story had been, its owner had always concluded mysteriously smartly that that was the hand of God at work; and thus was not to be stopped by anyone.

She had helped a few get back home. She would listen to the story of this one and see what to do about it.

For Miss Pheromone, there was no turning back. She had received a calling and she would live it out with all her strength and gifts. She would sing; arrange the church for the holy service; speak only holy words to the people of God; and just serve, serve and serve God some more. It was all there was to this life under the sun, really.

So, she became Sister Fenny. Sister Fenny, in a brown habit and white headscarf that fell and spread graciously upon her back, now attracted people to God. They looked at the uncovered portions of her stunning face. They beheld her bright eyes that were yet so full of life. They listened with relish to her polished language. With pleasure they listened to her voice rising and falling, filling the giant Fountain Church as she praised God in song. Everything about Sister Fenny pleased them absolutely. Many a man wished to grab her from the convent; but no, they could not. She continued to serve the Lord.

THE END!

Make Notes Here: